Judy the Bad Fairy

Written by
MARTIN WADDELL

Illustrated by
DOM MANSELL

WALKER BOOKS
LONDON

Judy was a lazy fairy.

She worked very hard at it.

While all the other fairies were dashing about *doing* or dancing in the dell, Judy hung there in a honeysuckle hammock drinking buttercup wine.

The other fairies got mad at her. They had a meeting.

"Get Judy a job!" they told the Fairy Queen.

"No fear!" muttered Judy, huddling down in her hammock.

"JUDY!" roared the Fairy Queen.

"Oh, okay!" said Judy, flopping out of her hammock.

"Go and do some DOINGS, JUDY!" ordered the Fairy Queen. Judy went off to do them. She spotted six Princes…

and changed them into frogs,
just like that, right in front of
their Princesses.
"Drat that!" cried the six Princesses,
and they complained to their Dad
and Mum, the Real King and Queen.
The Real King and Queen were cross,
because all the Princesses were crying.

The Real Queen got on the telephone to the Good Fairies, to complain. The Good Fairies did some quick frog-changes, and then they charged off to tell the Fairy Queen.

The Fairy Queen was very angry with Judy.

"I was only doing my job," Judy said.

"No need to overdo it!" said the Fairy Queen, huffily. "One Prince at a time is quite sufficient!"

"Judy's a bad fairy!" all the Good Fairies cried.

"Right!" said the Fairy Queen. "Be a bad fairy then, Judy, if that's all you're good at."

Judy went down to the Fairy Stores and collected a
sewing machine, and then she nipped off to the tallest
tower in the Real King and Queen's castle and set up a
sewing circle.

The six Princesses were just getting over frog-shock
when they heard about it, and they rushed upstairs to
join. They weren't very bright, just rich and beautiful.
They weren't very good at sewing either. They all pricked
their fingers. Soon there were Princesses sleeping all
over the place.

Sewing Circle

The Real King and Queen wailed in despair, and then they stopped wailing, and the Real Queen got on the telephone to the Good Fairies.

The Good Fairies got going, and undid all Judy's enchantments. Then they trooped off and complained to the Fairy Queen.

"Only doing my job!" said Judy. "Perhaps you'd better let me go back to my hammock?"

"No way!" said the Fairy Queen, who was getting pretty fed up with Judy. "Dart off down to the wood and try some fortune telling."

"If you insist, Ma'am!" said Judy politely. She fetched a crystal ball from the Fairy Stores, and went off to the deep dark wood, to wait for passing Knights Errant.

It was a busy day in the wood, with lots of Knights Erranting about. They all crossed Judy's palm with silver, and she told *all* of them that they were going to be Kings, and marry Princesses.

"Whoopee!" cried the Knights Errant, and they bought silver swords from Judy and set off to besiege the nearest castle, which belonged to You-Know-Who.

The Real King heard all the fighting and hid under the bedclothes. He was dead scared. But the Real Queen was a good fighter. That's how she got to be queen in the first place. She put on her second-best armour and clanked out of the castle.

WHAM! WHACK! BAM! ZOWEE!

The Real Queen laid about her. She made mincemeat of the Knights Errant. Legs and bits got chopped off right left and centre, and made a terrible mess in the moat.

When the fight was over, the Real King got out of bed and came down to take a look. "My roses are ruined," he cried, gnashing his flowerpots.

"So sorry, dear," said the Real Queen.

"They must be avenged," said the Real King.

Luckily, none of the Knights Errant had cut the telephone wires, so the Real Queen rang the Good Fairies. The Good Fairies got busy and turned the surviving Knights Errant into toadstools. And the Real King was delighted. Some of the Princesses were very upset, but nobody listened to them. They had enough Princes to go on with anyway. The Good Fairies dashed back to the Dell, to complain to the Fairy Queen.

"Not Judy AGAIN!" roared the Fairy Queen.

"Yes, Judy again!" said the Good Fairies, who were tired out with all the exercise they were getting.

"Only doing my job!" said Judy. "Just nip back into my hammock, shall I?"

The Fairy Queen had a Good Long Think, and then she snapped her fingers and said, "TEETH!"

"Teeth?" said Judy, halfway to the hammock.

"I'm putting you on teeth!" the Fairy Queen snapped. "You can be Tooth Fairy for the Realm. There's your Toothbag, and there's your Under-the-Pillow Money. Bring back at least fourteen teeth each night at midnight, OR ELSE!"

Fourteen teeth is a lot of teeth.

Poor Judy had to scoot about. Most of the poor people had no teeth, or very black ones, so by and large she stuck to the Castle.

Most of the people in the castle had bedrooms at the top of the tall towers. Upstairs and downstairs ran Judy, top speed, teeth-gathering and money-under-pillow-dumping..

"I've fixed her this time!" said the Fairy Queen delightedly. And all the Good Fairies held a Fairy Party in the Dell to celebrate, and took turns in Judy's honeysuckle hammock.

Judy got so tired that her Fairy Legs wouldn't work any more. She sank down halfway up the tallest tower, and lay there like a dead Fairy.

Then…

SNORE! SNORE! SNORE! SNORE!
The Snoring was coming from behind
a door. Judy opened it, looking
for somewhere to lie down. And…
it was the King's Aunty Chamber!
All the King's Aunties were asleep
there. Each one had a little bed
all to herself, and beside each
little bed there was a little table,
and on each little table there was
a little glass, and in each little
glass was…

a set of TEETH!

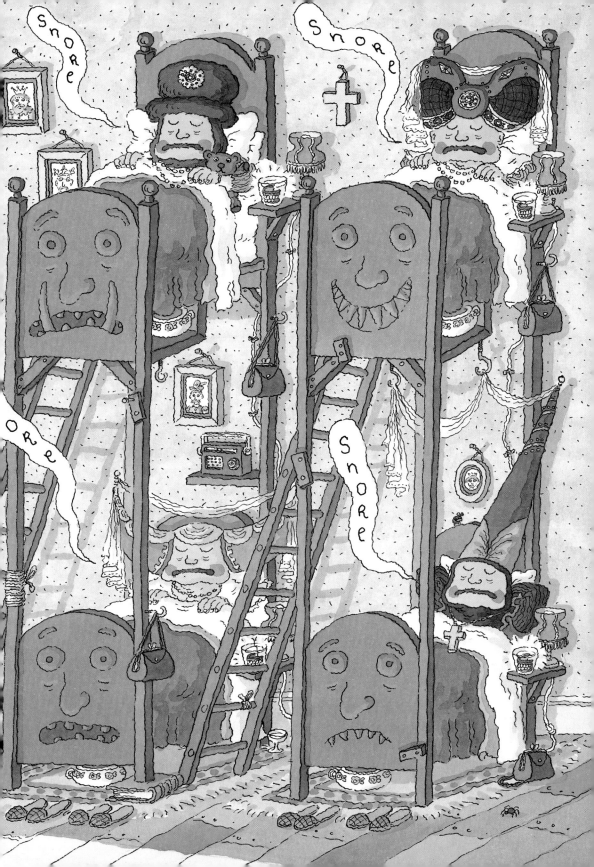

Judy nabbed the nearest.

There were twenty-eight teeth in it, which meant Judy was able to take the weekend off in the honeysuckle hammock, and still hand in fourteen teeth each night at the stroke of twelve.

The Aunty who had lost her teeth was very cross. She went around going

WOFF WOFF WOFF

because she had no teeth in, but of course nobody could understand her. So nothing happened. Nobody told the Real King or the Real Queen, and there were no telephone calls to the Good Fairies.

On the Monday night, after her weekend off, Judy went back to the Aunty Chamber and cleared the lot. *All* the King's Aunties woke up in the morning and found that they had no teeth.

"Woff woff woff," went all the Aunties.

The Real King and Queen couldn't understand a word. Then all the Aunties demanded soup and soft vegetables for dinner, and refused to say "Please" and "Thank you."

The Aunties had always been very polite, so the Real King and Queen knew that something Awful Was Up!

The Real Queen telephoned the Good Fairies. The Good
Fairies got on the job, and magicked all the teeth back,
although they didn't get the pillow money back because
the Aunties had spent it.

The Good Fairies were really furious and they
told the Fairy Queen about it.

"JUDY!" roared the Fairy Queen.

"I was only doing my job!" said Judy.

"Well, you're *not* to do jobs any more!" said the
Fairy Queen. "You cause too much trouble. I banish you
back to your hammock. Get in it and don't get out!"

"Oh good!" said Judy.

GO!

Honeysuckle Hammock
This way...

All the Fairies were pleased, and so were the Real King and Queen up at the Castle, and the Princes and Princesses, and everybody else, except the Knights Errant, who went on being toadstools. And Judy lived happily ever after in her honeysuckle hammock, undisturbed by the doings in the Dell.

end.

THE END